THE 94-DAY ASCENSION MANIFESTATION JOURNAL

A JOURNEY TO CONFIDENCE, SUCCESS, AND ABUNDANCE

NEELIMA DAVULURI

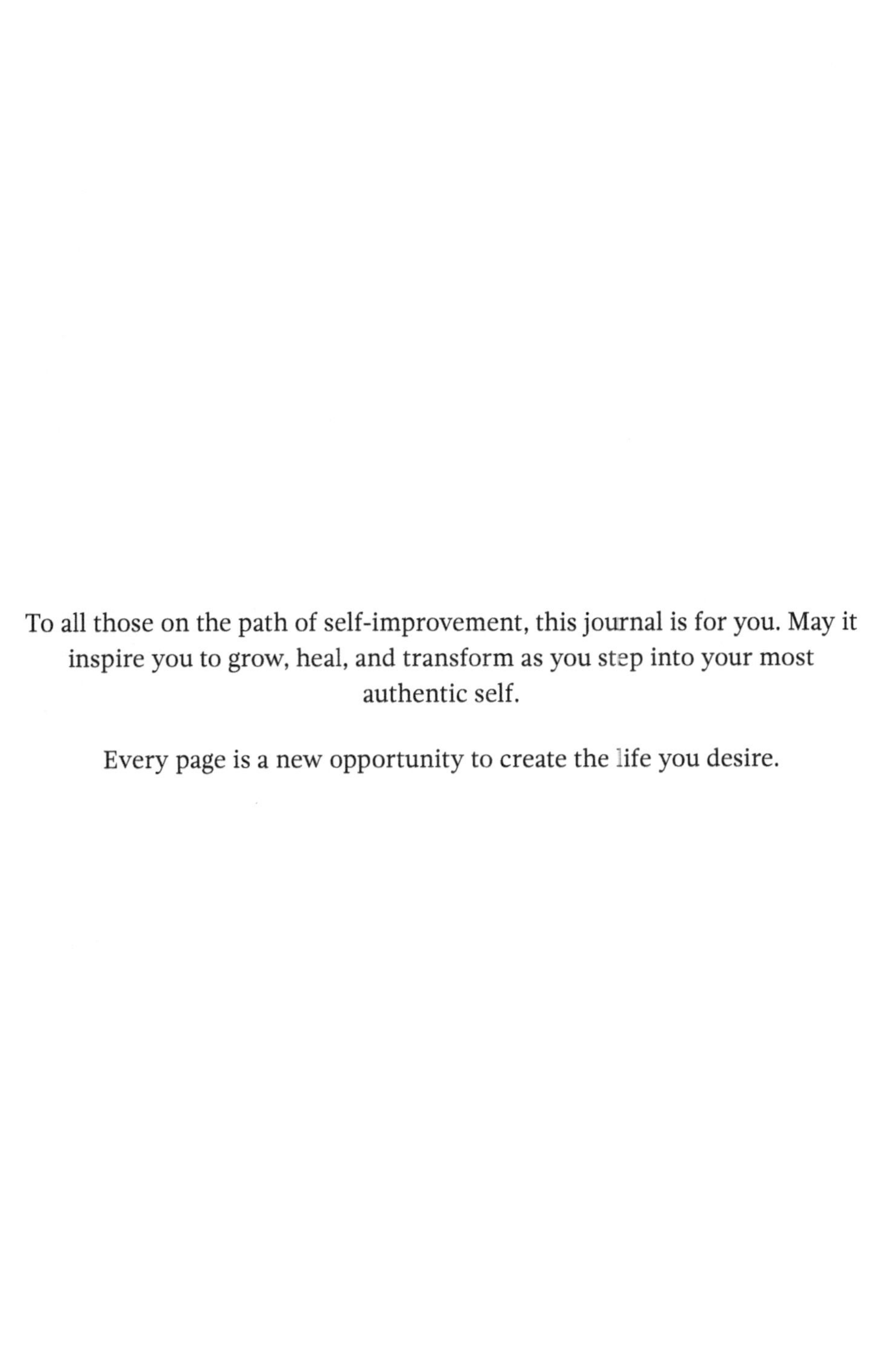

To all those on the path of self-improvement, this journal is for you. May it inspire you to grow, heal, and transform as you step into your most authentic self.

Every page is a new opportunity to create the life you desire.

Contents

Contents

Contents

Contents

Foreword

Welcome to 'The 94-Day Ascension,' a journal designed to guide you through 94 days of manifestation. In this journey, you'll align your thoughts, intentions, and actions to move closer to the life you envision. By the end, you will embody the confidence, success, contentment, and abundance that you seek.

The 94-Day Ascension: A Journey to Confidence, Success, and Abundance was born from my own personal need for transformation. In my quest for growth, I realized that the key to manifesting the life I wanted—full of confidence, success, and inner peace—was a structured, intentional approach. I created this journal as a tool to guide myself through the daily practice of setting intentions, reflecting on progress, and aligning with my goals. What started as a personal journey has evolved into something I felt compelled to share with others, knowing how powerful these simple yet consistent practices can be.

This is not just any journal; it's your personal companion for the next 94 days. I invite you to use it to explore your deepest desires, release what no longer serves you, and align with your highest self. As you embark on this journey, remember that transformation takes time, but with daily dedication, the life you dream of will unfold before you. I'm honored to share this tool with you and to be part of your ascension to confidence, contentment, and abundance.

Preface

The Power of 94 Days

Why 94 Days? It's a question that might come to mind for many readers. The answer lies in the transformative power of consistent effort over time. 94 days is not just a random number—it's a carefully chosen period that allows for real, lasting change. It provides enough time to break old patterns, establish new habits, and fully align with your goals, all while giving you the space to reflect, grow, and ascend into your most authentic self.

The number **94 days** is specific, yet achievable, making it symbolic of both commitment and tangible progress. It gives readers a concrete time frame to focus on:

- **Long Enough for Real Change**: Studies suggest it takes about 90 days to establish meaningful habits. The 94-day period provides the structure and consistency needed for lasting transformation, going beyond superficial changes to create deep, personal growth.
- **Countdown to a New Year**: Since your journal counts down to the New Year, the 94 days becomes a reflective journey that closes one chapter and opens a new, more empowered phase of life.

Ascension implies rising or elevating oneself to a higher level—physically, mentally, emotionally, and spiritually.

The journal's goal is to guide readers toward becoming more **confident, content, successful,** and **abundant** by the end of the 94 days.

Over the course of 94 days, the readers will ascend to a higher state of being and aligned with their true purpose.

How To Use This Journal

1. **What is Manifestation?**
   Manifestation is the practice of bringing your goals, desires, and dreams into reality by focusing on positive thoughts, emotions, and actions. The law of attraction states that whatever you focus on expands, so if you focus on success, confidence, and abundance, these qualities will manifest in your life.

2. **How to Write Affirmations**
   Affirmations are positive statements that declare what you want to manifest as if it's already happening. Some tips for writing affirmations:

   - Start with "I am" or "I have" to state your intention in the present tense.
   - Keep it positive (e.g., "I am confident," instead of "I am not insecure").
   - Be specific, but simple enough to be easily repeated.
   - Feel the emotion behind your words.

3. **Using Visualization & Intention Setting**
   Visualization is the process of imagining your desired outcomes in vivid detail.

   - Close your eyes and picture yourself living the life you want.
   - See, hear, and feel what it's like to already have what you're manifesting.
   - After visualization, write down specific intentions for the day that align with your goals.

4. **Gratitude Practice**
   Gratitude is a powerful tool for manifestation. By focusing on what you're grateful for, you shift your mindset to abundance.

   - Write down three things you're grateful for each day, no matter how small.
   - This practice will help you attract more things to be grateful for.

5. **Daily Action Towards Goals**
   Manifestation requires both mindset and action. Each day, identify one action that aligns with your goals, and take it with purpose and confidence.

6. **Evening Reflection**
   End each day by reflecting on your wins and progress. Acknowledge the small victories and any signs that your manifestation is working. This will keep you motivated and focused on your journey.

CHAPTER I

Day 1

"You are never too old to set another goal or to dream a new dream." – C.S. Lewis

Morning Affirmations

Write 5 affirmations as you start the day. (A few suggestions for affirmations as below)

"I am worthy of success and abundance."
"I trust in the process of life."
"I release all fear and embrace confidence."

1. ____
2. ____
3. ____
4. ____
5. ____

Visualization & Intention Setting

Spend 5-10 minutes visualizing yourself as the confident, successful, abundant person you're becoming.

Today's Intentions:

1. ____
2. ____
3. ____

Gratitude Practice

List 3 things you're grateful for today:

1. ____
2. ____
3. ____

Daily Action Towards Goals

What is one action you can take today that aligns with your goals?

____

Evening Reflection & Acknowledgment

How did you feel today? What did you accomplish? Any signs of manifestation?

____

Small Wins:

____

• • •

CHAPTER II

Day 2

"Believe you can and you're halfway there." –
Theodore Roosevelt

Morning Affirmations

Write 5 affirmations as you start the day. (A few suggestions for affirmations as below)
   "I am worthy of success and abundance."
   "I trust in the process of life."
   "I release all fear and embrace confidence."
   1. ____
   2. ____
   3. ____
   4. ____
   5. ____

Visualization & Intention Setting

Spend 5-10 minutes visualizing yourself as the confident, successful, abundant person you're becoming.
   Today's Intentions:
   1. ____
   2. ____
   3. ____

Gratitude Practice

List 3 things you're grateful for today:

1. ____
2. ____
3. ____

Daily Action Towards Goals

What is one action you can take today that aligns with your goals?

____

Evening Reflection & Acknowledgment

How did you feel today? What did you accomplish? Any signs of manifestation?

____

Small Wins:

____

CHAPTER III

Day 3

"Start where you are. Use what you have. Do what you can." – Arthur Ashe

Morning Affirmations

Write 5 affirmations as you start the day. (A few suggestions for affirmations as below)

"I am worthy of success and abundance."
"I trust in the process of life."
"I release all fear and embrace confidence."

1. ______________________________________
2. ______________________________________
3. ______________________________________
4. ______________________________________
5. ______________________________________

Visualization & Intention Setting

Spend 5-10 minutes visualizing yourself as the confident, successful, abundant person you're becoming.

Today's Intentions:

1. ______________________________________
2. ______________________________________
3. ______________________________________

Gratitude Practice

List 3 things you're grateful for today:

1. ____
2. ____
3. ____

Daily Action Towards Goals

What is one action you can take today that aligns with your goals?

____

Evening Reflection & Acknowledgment

How did you feel today? What did you accomplish? Any signs of manifestation?

____

Small Wins:

____

CHAPTER IV

Day 4

"Act as if what you do makes a difference. It does." – William James

Morning Affirmations

Write 5 affirmations as you start the day. (A few suggestions for affirmations as below)

"I am worthy of success and abundance."
"I trust in the process of life."
"I release all fear and embrace confidence."

1. ____
2. ____
3. ____
4. ____
5. ____

Visualization & Intention Setting

Spend 5-10 minutes visualizing yourself as the confident, successful, abundant person you're becoming.

Today's Intentions:

1. ____
2. ____
3. ____

Gratitude Practice

List 3 things you're grateful for today:

1. ____
2. ____
3. ____

Daily Action Towards Goals

What is one action you can take today that aligns with your goals?

____

Evening Reflection & Acknowledgment

How did you feel today? What did you accomplish? Any signs of manifestation?

____

Small Wins:

____

CHAPTER V

Day 5

"Hardships often prepare ordinary people for an extraordinary destiny." – C.S. Lewis

Morning Affirmations

Write 5 affirmations as you start the day. (A few suggestions for affirmations as below)

"I am worthy of success and abundance."
"I trust in the process of life."
"I release all fear and embrace confidence."

1. ____
2. ____
3. ____
4. ____
5. ____

Visualization & Intention Setting

Spend 5-10 minutes visualizing yourself as the confident, successful, abundant person you're becoming.

Today's Intentions:

1. ____
2. ____
3. ____

Gratitude Practice

List 3 things you're grateful for today:

1. ____
2. ____
3. ____

Daily Action Towards Goals

What is one action you can take today that aligns with your goals?

____

Evening Reflection & Acknowledgment

How did you feel today? What did you accomplish? Any signs of manifestation?

____

Small Wins:

____

CHAPTER VI

Day 6

"The only way to achieve the impossible is to believe it is possible." – Charles Kingsleigh

Morning Affirmations

Write 5 affirmations as you start the day. (A few suggestions for affirmations as below)

"I am worthy of success and abundance."
"I trust in the process of life."
"I release all fear and embrace confidence."

1. _______________________________________
2. _______________________________________
3. _______________________________________
4. _______________________________________
5. _______________________________________

Visualization & Intention Setting

Spend 5-10 minutes visualizing yourself as the confident, successful, abundant person you're becoming.

Today's Intentions:

1. _______________________________________
2. _______________________________________
3. _______________________________________

Gratitude Practice

List 3 things you're grateful for today:

1. ______________________________________
2. ______________________________________
3. ______________________________________

Daily Action Towards Goals

What is one action you can take today that aligns with your goals?

____

Evening Reflection & Acknowledgment

How did you feel today? What did you accomplish? Any signs of manifestation?

____

Small Wins:

____

CHAPTER VII

Day 7

"Don't watch the clock; do what it does. Keep going." – Sam Levenson

Morning Affirmations

Write 5 affirmations as you start the day. (A few suggestions for affirmations as below)

"I am worthy of success and abundance."
"I trust in the process of life."
"I release all fear and embrace confidence."

1. ____
2. ____
3. ____
4. ____
5. ____

Visualization & Intention Setting

Spend 5-10 minutes visualizing yourself as the confident, successful, abundant person you're becoming.

Today's Intentions:

1. ____
2. ____
3. ____

Gratitude Practice

List 3 things you're grateful for today:

1. _______________________________________
2. _______________________________________
3. _______________________________________

Daily Action Towards Goals

What is one action you can take today that aligns with your goals?

____

Evening Reflection & Acknowledgment

How did you feel today? What did you accomplish? Any signs of manifestation?

____

Small Wins:

____

CHAPTER VIII

Day 8

"Don't be afraid to give up the good to go for the great." – John D. Rockefeller

Morning Affirmations

Write 5 affirmations as you start the day. (A few suggestions for affirmations as below)

"I am worthy of success and abundance."
"I trust in the process of life."
"I release all fear and embrace confidence."

1. _______________________________________
2. _______________________________________
3. _______________________________________
4. _______________________________________
5. _______________________________________

Visualization & Intention Setting

Spend 5-10 minutes visualizing yourself as the confident, successful, abundant person you're becoming.

Today's Intentions:

1. _______________________________________
2. _______________________________________
3. _______________________________________

Gratitude Practice

List 3 things you're grateful for today:

1. _______________________________________
2. _______________________________________
3. _______________________________________

Daily Action Towards Goals

What is one action you can take today that aligns with your goals?

____

Evening Reflection & Acknowledgment

How did you feel today? What did you accomplish? Any signs of manifestation?

____

Small Wins:

____

CHAPTER IX

Day 9

*"Opportunities don't happen. You create them." –
Chris Grosser*

Morning Affirmations

Write 5 affirmations as you start the day. (A few suggestions for affirmations as below)
"I am worthy of success and abundance."
"I trust in the process of life."
"I release all fear and embrace confidence."

1. _______________________________________
2. _______________________________________
3. _______________________________________
4. _______________________________________
5. _______________________________________

Visualization & Intention Setting

Spend 5-10 minutes visualizing yourself as the confident, successful, abundant person you're becoming.

Today's Intentions:

1. _______________________________________
2. _______________________________________
3. _______________________________________

Gratitude Practice

List 3 things you're grateful for today:

1. ____
2. ____
3. ____

Daily Action Towards Goals

What is one action you can take today that aligns with your goals?

____

Evening Reflection & Acknowledgment

How did you feel today? What did you accomplish? Any signs of manifestation?

____

Small Wins:

____

CHAPTER X

Day 10

"Everything you've ever wanted is on the other side of fear." – George Addair

Morning Affirmations

Write 5 affirmations as you start the day. (A few suggestions for affirmations as below)

"I am worthy of success and abundance."
"I trust in the process of life."
"I release all fear and embrace confidence."

1. ____
2. ____
3. ____
4. ____
5. ____

Visualization & Intention Setting

Spend 5-10 minutes visualizing yourself as the confident, successful, abundant person you're becoming.

Today's Intentions:

1. ____
2. ____
3. ____

Gratitude Practice

List 3 things you're grateful for today:

1. ____________________________________
2. ____________________________________
3. ____________________________________

Daily Action Towards Goals

What is one action you can take today that aligns with your goals?

____

Evening Reflection & Acknowledgment

How did you feel today? What did you accomplish? Any signs of manifestation?

____

Small Wins:

____

CHAPTER XI

Day 11

"It's not whether you get knocked down, it's whether you get up." – Vince Lombardi

Morning Affirmations

Write 5 affirmations as you start the day. (A few suggestions for affirmations as below)

"I am worthy of success and abundance."
"I trust in the process of life."
"I release all fear and embrace confidence."

1. ____
2. ____
3. ____
4. ____
5. ____

Visualization & Intention Setting

Spend 5-10 minutes visualizing yourself as the confident, successful, abundant person you're becoming.

Today's Intentions:

1. ____
2. ____
3. ____

Gratitude Practice

List 3 things you're grateful for today:

1. ____
2. ____
3. ____

Daily Action Towards Goals

What is one action you can take today that aligns with your goals?
____

Evening Reflection & Acknowledgment

How did you feel today? What did you accomplish? Any signs of manifestation?
____

Small Wins:
____

CHAPTER XII

Day 12

"We generate fears while we sit. We overcome them by action." – Dr. Henry Link

Morning Affirmations

Write 5 affirmations as you start the day. (A few suggestions for affirmations as below)

"I am worthy of success and abundance."
"I trust in the process of life."
"I release all fear and embrace confidence."

1. ____
2. ____
3. ____
4. ____
5. ____

Visualization & Intention Setting

Spend 5-10 minutes visualizing yourself as the confident, successful, abundant person you're becoming.

Today's Intentions:

1. ____
2. ____
3. ____

Gratitude Practice

List 3 things you're grateful for today:

1. _______________________________________
2. _______________________________________
3. _______________________________________

Daily Action Towards Goals

What is one action you can take today that aligns with your goals?

____

Evening Reflection & Acknowledgment

How did you feel today? What did you accomplish? Any signs of manifestation?

____

Small Wins:

____

CHAPTER XIII

Day 13

"Success is walking from failure to failure with no loss of enthusiasm." – Winston Churchill

Morning Affirmations

Write 5 affirmations as you start the day. (A few suggestions for affirmations as below)

"I am worthy of success and abundance."
"I trust in the process of life."
"I release all fear and embrace confidence."

1. ____
2. ____
3. ____
4. ____
5. ____

Visualization & Intention Setting

Spend 5-10 minutes visualizing yourself as the confident, successful, abundant person you're becoming.

Today's Intentions:

1. ____
2. ____
3. ____

Gratitude Practice

List 3 things you're grateful for today:

1. ______________________________
2. ______________________________
3. ______________________________

Daily Action Towards Goals

What is one action you can take today that aligns with your goals?

____

Evening Reflection & Acknowledgment

How did you feel today? What did you accomplish? Any signs of manifestation?

____

Small Wins:

____

CHAPTER XIV

Day 14

"It does not matter how slowly you go, as long as you do not stop." – Confucius

Morning Affirmations

Write 5 affirmations as you start the day. (A few suggestions for affirmations as below)

"I am worthy of success and abundance."
"I trust in the process of life."
"I release all fear and embrace confidence."

1. ____
2. ____
3. ____
4. ____
5. ____

Visualization & Intention Setting

Spend 5-10 minutes visualizing yourself as the confident, successful, abundant person you're becoming.

Today's Intentions:

1. ____
2. ____
3. ____

Gratitude Practice

List 3 things you're grateful for today:

1. ____
2. ____
3. ____

Daily Action Towards Goals

What is one action you can take today that aligns with your goals?

____

Evening Reflection & Acknowledgment

How did you feel today? What did you accomplish? Any signs of manifestation?

____

Small Wins:

____

CHAPTER XV

Day 15

*"I never dreamed about success, I worked for it." –
Estee Lauder*

Morning Affirmations

Write 5 affirmations as you start the day. (A few suggestions for affirmations as below)

"I am worthy of success and abundance."
"I trust in the process of life."
"I release all fear and embrace confidence."

1. ____
2. ____
3. ____
4. ____
5. ____

Visualization & Intention Setting

Spend 5-10 minutes visualizing yourself as the confident, successful, abundant person you're becoming.

Today's Intentions:

1. ____
2. ____
3. ____

Gratitude Practice

List 3 things you're grateful for today:

1. ____
2. ____
3. ____

Daily Action Towards Goals

What is one action you can take today that aligns with your goals?

____

Evening Reflection & Acknowledgment

How did you feel today? What did you accomplish? Any signs of manifestation?

____

Small Wins:

____

CHAPTER XVI

Day 16

"It is never too late to be what you might have been." – George Eliot

Morning Affirmations

Write 5 affirmations as you start the day. (A few suggestions for affirmations as below)

"I am worthy of success and abundance."
"I trust in the process of life."
"I release all fear and embrace confidence."

1. ____
2. ____
3. ____
4. ____
5. ____

Visualization & Intention Setting

Spend 5-10 minutes visualizing yourself as the confident, successful, abundant person you're becoming.

Today's Intentions:

1. ____
2. ____
3. ____

Gratitude Practice

List 3 things you're grateful for today:

1. ____
2. ____
3. ____

Daily Action Towards Goals

What is one action you can take today that aligns with your goals?

____

Evening Reflection & Acknowledgment

How did you feel today? What did you accomplish? Any signs of manifestation?

____

Small Wins:

____

CHAPTER XVII

Day 17

"You are not a drop in the ocean. You are the entire ocean in a drop." - Rumi

Morning Affirmations

Write 5 affirmations as you start the day. (A few suggestions for affirmations as below)

"I am worthy of success and abundance."
"I trust in the process of life."
"I release all fear and embrace confidence."

1. ____
2. ____
3. ____
4. ____
5. ____

Visualization & Intention Setting

Spend 5-10 minutes visualizing yourself as the confident, successful, abundant person you're becoming.

Today's Intentions:

1. ____
2. ____
3. ____

Gratitude Practice

List 3 things you're grateful for today:

1. ____
2. ____
3. ____

Daily Action Towards Goals

What is one action you can take today that aligns with your goals?

____

Evening Reflection & Acknowledgment

How did you feel today? What did you accomplish? Any signs of manifestation?

____

Small Wins:

____

CHAPTER XVIII

Day 18

"Happiness is not something ready-made. It comes from your own actions." – Dalai Lama

Morning Affirmations

Write 5 affirmations as you start the day. (A few suggestions for affirmations as below)

"I am worthy of success and abundance."
"I trust in the process of life."
"I release all fear and embrace confidence."

1. ____
2. ____
3. ____
4. ____
5. ____

Visualization & Intention Setting

Spend 5-10 minutes visualizing yourself as the confident, successful, abundant person you're becoming.

Today's Intentions:

1. ____
2. ____
3. ____

Gratitude Practice

List 3 things you're grateful for today:

1. _______________________________________
2. _______________________________________
3. _______________________________________

Daily Action Towards Goals

What is one action you can take today that aligns with your goals?

____

Evening Reflection & Acknowledgment

How did you feel today? What did you accomplish? Any signs of manifestation?

____

Small Wins:

____

CHAPTER XIX

Day 19

"You are enough just as you are." – Bridgett Jones

Morning Affirmations

Write 5 affirmations as you start the day. (A few suggestions for affirmations as below)

"I am worthy of success and abundance."
"I trust in the process of life."
"I release all fear and embrace confidence."

1. _______________________________________
2. _______________________________________
3. _______________________________________
4. _______________________________________
5. _______________________________________

Visualization & Intention Setting

Spend 5-10 minutes visualizing yourself as the confident, successful, abundant person you're becoming.

Today's Intentions:

1. _______________________________________
2. _______________________________________
3. _______________________________________

Gratitude Practice

List 3 things you're grateful for today:

1. _______________________________________

2. _______________________________________
3. _______________________________________

Daily Action Towards Goals

What is one action you can take today that aligns with your goals?

____

Evening Reflection & Acknowledgment

How did you feel today? What did you accomplish? Any signs of manifestation?

____

Small Wins:

____

CHAPTER XX

Day 20

"In the middle of every difficulty lies opportunity."
– Albert Einstein

Morning Affirmations

Write 5 affirmations as you start the day. (A few suggestions for affirmations as below)

"I am worthy of success and abundance."
"I trust in the process of life."
"I release all fear and embrace confidence."

1. ____
2. ____
3. ____
4. ____
5. ____

Visualization & Intention Setting

Spend 5-10 minutes visualizing yourself as the confident, successful, abundant person you're becoming.

Today's Intentions:

1. ____
2. ____
3. ____

Gratitude Practice

List 3 things you're grateful for today:

1. _______________________________________
2. _______________________________________
3. _______________________________________

Daily Action Towards Goals

What is one action you can take today that aligns with your goals?

____

Evening Reflection & Acknowledgment

How did you feel today? What did you accomplish? Any signs of manifestation?

____

Small Wins:

____

CHAPTER XXI

Day 21

"Don't stop when you're tired. Stop when you're done." – Unknown

Morning Affirmations

Write 5 affirmations as you start the day. (A few suggestions for affirmations as below)

"I am worthy of success and abundance."
"I trust in the process of life."
"I release all fear and embrace confidence."

1. ____
2. ____
3. ____
4. ____
5. ____

Visualization & Intention Setting

Spend 5-10 minutes visualizing yourself as the confident, successful, abundant person you're becoming.

Today's Intentions:

1. ____
2. ____
3. ____

Gratitude Practice

List 3 things you're grateful for today:

1. _______________________________________
2. _______________________________________
3. _______________________________________

Daily Action Towards Goals

What is one action you can take today that aligns with your goals?

____

Evening Reflection & Acknowledgment

How did you feel today? What did you accomplish? Any signs of manifestation?

____

Small Wins:

____

CHAPTER XXII

Day 22

"Dream it. Wish it. Do it." – Unknown

Morning Affirmations

Write 5 affirmations as you start the day. (A few suggestions for affirmations as below)

"I am worthy of success and abundance."
"I trust in the process of life."
"I release all fear and embrace confidence."

1. ____
2. ____
3. ____
4. ____
5. ____

Visualization & Intention Setting

Spend 5-10 minutes visualizing yourself as the confident, successful, abundant person you're becoming.

Today's Intentions:

1. ____
2. ____
3. ____

Gratitude Practice

List 3 things you're grateful for today:

1. ____

2. _______________________________________
3. _______________________________________

Daily Action Towards Goals

What is one action you can take today that aligns with your goals?

____

Evening Reflection & Acknowledgment

How did you feel today? What did you accomplish? Any signs of manifestation?

____

Small Wins:

____

CHAPTER XXIII

Day 23

"Doubt kills more dreams than failure ever will." –
Suzy Kassem

Morning Affirmations

Write 5 affirmations as you start the day. (A few suggestions for affirmations as below)
   "I am worthy of success and abundance."
   "I trust in the process of life."
   "I release all fear and embrace confidence."
   1. ____
   2. ____
   3. ____
   4. ____
   5. ____

Visualization & Intention Setting

Spend 5-10 minutes visualizing yourself as the confident, successful, abundant person you're becoming.
   Today's Intentions:
   1. ____
   2. ____
   3. ____

Gratitude Practice

List 3 things you're grateful for today:

1. ____
2. ____
3. ____

Daily Action Towards Goals

What is one action you can take today that aligns with your goals?

____

Evening Reflection & Acknowledgment

How did you feel today? What did you accomplish? Any signs of manifestation?

____

Small Wins:

____

CHAPTER XXIV

Day 24

"All our dreams can come true if we have the courage to pursue them." – Walt Disney

Morning Affirmations

Write 5 affirmations as you start the day. (A few suggestions for affirmations as below)

"I am worthy of success and abundance."
"I trust in the process of life."
"I release all fear and embrace confidence."

1. ____
2. ____
3. ____
4. ____
5. ____

Visualization & Intention Setting

Spend 5-10 minutes visualizing yourself as the confident, successful, abundant person you're becoming.

Today's Intentions:

1. ____
2. ____
3. ____

Gratitude Practice

List 3 things you're grateful for today:

1. _______________________________________
2. _______________________________________
3. _______________________________________

Daily Action Towards Goals

What is one action you can take today that aligns with your goals?

____

Evening Reflection & Acknowledgment

How did you feel today? What did you accomplish? Any signs of manifestation?

____

Small Wins:

____

CHAPTER XXV

Day 25

"To be a champion, you have to believe in yourself when nobody else will." – Sugar Ray Robinson

Morning Affirmations

Write 5 affirmations as you start the day. (A few suggestions for affirmations as below)
   "I am worthy of success and abundance."
   "I trust in the process of life."
   "I release all fear and embrace confidence."
   1. ____
   2. ____
   3. ____
   4. ____
   5. ____

Visualization & Intention Setting

Spend 5-10 minutes visualizing yourself as the confident, successful, abundant person you're becoming.
   Today's Intentions:
   1. ____
   2. ____
   3. ____

Gratitude Practice

List 3 things you're grateful for today:

1. ____
2. ____
3. ____

Daily Action Towards Goals

What is one action you can take today that aligns with your goals?

____

Evening Reflection & Acknowledgment

How did you feel today? What did you accomplish? Any signs of manifestation?

____

Small Wins:

____

CHAPTER XXVI

Day 26

"If you want something you've never had, you must be willing to do something you've never done." – Thomas Jefferson

Morning Affirmations

Write 5 affirmations as you start the day. (A few suggestions for affirmations as below)

"I am worthy of success and abundance."
"I trust in the process of life."
"I release all fear and embrace confidence."

1. ____
2. ____
3. ____
4. ____
5. ____

Visualization & Intention Setting

Spend 5-10 minutes visualizing yourself as the confident, successful, abundant person you're becoming.

Today's Intentions:

1. ____
2. ____
3. ____

Gratitude Practice

List 3 things you're grateful for today:

1. ____

2. ____

3. ____

Daily Action Towards Goals

What is one action you can take today that aligns with your goals?

____

Evening Reflection & Acknowledgment

How did you feel today? What did you accomplish? Any signs of manifestation?

____

Small Wins:

____

CHAPTER XXVII

Day 27

"Don't limit your challenges, challenge your limits." – Jerry Dunn

Morning Affirmations

Write 5 affirmations as you start the day. (A few suggestions for affirmations as below)
"I am worthy of success and abundance."
"I trust in the process of life."
"I release all fear and embrace confidence."

1. ____
2. ____
3. ____
4. ____
5. ____

Visualization & Intention Setting

Spend 5-10 minutes visualizing yourself as the confident, successful, abundant person you're becoming.

Today's Intentions:

1. ____
2. ____
3. ____

Gratitude Practice

List 3 things you're grateful for today:

1. ____
2. ____
3. ____

Daily Action Towards Goals

What is one action you can take today that aligns with your goals?

____

Evening Reflection & Acknowledgment

How did you feel today? What did you accomplish? Any signs of manifestation?

____

Small Wins:

____

CHAPTER XXVIII

Day 28

"A goal without a plan is just a wish." – Antoine de Saint-Exupéry

Morning Affirmations

Write 5 affirmations as you start the day. (A few suggestions for affirmations as below)

"I am worthy of success and abundance."
"I trust in the process of life."
"I release all fear and embrace confidence."

1. ____
2. ____
3. ____
4. ____
5. ____

Visualization & Intention Setting

Spend 5-10 minutes visualizing yourself as the confident, successful, abundant person you're becoming.

Today's Intentions:

1. ____
2. ____
3. ____

Gratitude Practice

List 3 things you're grateful for today:

1. ______________________________________
2. ______________________________________
3. ______________________________________

Daily Action Towards Goals

What is one action you can take today that aligns with your goals?

____

Evening Reflection & Acknowledgment

How did you feel today? What did you accomplish? Any signs of manifestation?

____

Small Wins:

____

CHAPTER XXIX

Day 29

"You are never too small to make a difference." –
Greta Thunberg

Morning Affirmations

Write 5 affirmations as you start the day. (A few suggestions for affirmations as below)

"I am worthy of success and abundance."
"I trust in the process of life."
"I release all fear and embrace confidence."

1. _______________________________________
2. _______________________________________
3. _______________________________________
4. _______________________________________
5. _______________________________________

Visualization & Intention Setting

Spend 5-10 minutes visualizing yourself as the confident, successful, abundant person you're becoming.

Today's Intentions:

1. _______________________________________
2. _______________________________________
3. _______________________________________

Gratitude Practice

List 3 things you're grateful for today:

1. _______________________________________
2. _______________________________________
3. _______________________________________

Daily Action Towards Goals

What is one action you can take today that aligns with your goals?

____

Evening Reflection & Acknowledgment

How did you feel today? What did you accomplish? Any signs of manifestation?

____

Small Wins:

____

CHAPTER XXX

Day 30

"Impossible is just an opinion." – Paulo Coelho

Morning Affirmations

Write 5 affirmations as you start the day. (A few suggestions for affirmations as below)

"I am worthy of success and abundance."
"I trust in the process of life."
"I release all fear and embrace confidence."

1. ____
2. ____
3. ____
4. ____
5. ____

Visualization & Intention Setting

Spend 5-10 minutes visualizing yourself as the confident, successful, abundant person you're becoming.

Today's Intentions:

1. ____
2. ____
3. ____

Gratitude Practice

List 3 things you're grateful for today:

1. ____

2. ____

3. ____

Daily Action Towards Goals

What is one action you can take today that aligns with your goals?

____

Evening Reflection & Acknowledgment

How did you feel today? What did you accomplish? Any signs of manifestation?

____

Small Wins:

____

CHAPTER XXXI

Day 31

"You are capable of amazing things." – Unknown

Morning Affirmations

Write 5 affirmations as you start the day. (A few suggestions for affirmations as below)

"I am worthy of success and abundance."
"I trust in the process of life."
"I release all fear and embrace confidence."

1. _______________________________________
2. _______________________________________
3. _______________________________________
4. _______________________________________
5. _______________________________________

Visualization & Intention Setting

Spend 5-10 minutes visualizing yourself as the confident, successful, abundant person you're becoming.

Today's Intentions:

1. _______________________________________
2. _______________________________________
3. _______________________________________

Gratitude Practice

List 3 things you're grateful for today:

1. _______________________________________

2. _______________________________________
3. _______________________________________

Daily Action Towards Goals

What is one action you can take today that aligns with your goals?

____

Evening Reflection & Acknowledgment

How did you feel today? What did you accomplish? Any signs of manifestation?

____

Small Wins:

____

CHAPTER XXXII

Day 32

"The mind is everything. What you think you become." – Buddha

Morning Affirmations

Write 5 affirmations as you start the day. (A few suggestions for affirmations as below)

"I am worthy of success and abundance."
"I trust in the process of life."
"I release all fear and embrace confidence."

1. ____
2. ____
3. ____
4. ____
5. ____

Visualization & Intention Setting

Spend 5-10 minutes visualizing yourself as the confident, successful, abundant person you're becoming.

Today's Intentions:

1. ____
2. ____
3. ____

Gratitude Practice

List 3 things you're grateful for today:

1. ____
2. ____
3. ____

Daily Action Towards Goals

What is one action you can take today that aligns with your goals?

____

Evening Reflection & Acknowledgment

How did you feel today? What did you accomplish? Any signs of manifestation?

____

Small Wins:

____

CHAPTER XXXIII

Day 33

"You are not your circumstances. You are your possibilities." - Oprah Winfrey

Morning Affirmations

Write 5 affirmations as you start the day. (A few suggestions for affirmations as below)

"I am worthy of success and abundance."
"I trust in the process of life."
"I release all fear and embrace confidence."

1. ____
2. ____
3. ____
4. ____
5. ____

Visualization & Intention Setting

Spend 5-10 minutes visualizing yourself as the confident, successful, abundant person you're becoming.

Today's Intentions:

1. ____
2. ____
3. ____

Gratitude Practice

List 3 things you're grateful for today:

1. _______________________________________
2. _______________________________________
3. _______________________________________

Daily Action Towards Goals

What is one action you can take today that aligns with your goals?

____

Evening Reflection & Acknowledgment

How did you feel today? What did you accomplish? Any signs of manifestation?

____

Small Wins:

____

CHAPTER XXXIV

Day 34

*Progress is progress, no matter how small." –
Unknown*

Morning Affirmations

Write 5 affirmations as you start the day. (A few suggestions for affirmations as below)

"I am worthy of success and abundance."
"I trust in the process of life."
"I release all fear and embrace confidence."

1. ____
2. ____
3. ____
4. ____
5. ____

Visualization & Intention Setting

Spend 5-10 minutes visualizing yourself as the confident, successful, abundant person you're becoming.

Today's Intentions:

1. ____
2. ____
3. ____

Gratitude Practice

List 3 things you're grateful for today:

1. ____
2. ____
3. ____

Daily Action Towards Goals

What is one action you can take today that aligns with your goals?

____

Evening Reflection & Acknowledgment

How did you feel today? What did you accomplish? Any signs of manifestation?

____

Small Wins:

____

CHAPTER XXXV

Day 35

"When you focus on the good, the good gets better." – Abraham Hicks

Morning Affirmations

Write 5 affirmations as you start the day. (A few suggestions for affirmations as below)

"I am worthy of success and abundance."
"I trust in the process of life."
"I release all fear and embrace confidence."

1. ____
2. ____
3. ____
4. ____
5. ____

Visualization & Intention Setting

Spend 5-10 minutes visualizing yourself as the confident, successful, abundant person you're becoming.

Today's Intentions:

1. ____
2. ____
3. ____

Gratitude Practice

List 3 things you're grateful for today:

1. _______________________________________
2. _______________________________________
3. _______________________________________

Daily Action Towards Goals

What is one action you can take today that aligns with your goals?

____

Evening Reflection & Acknowledgment

How did you feel today? What did you accomplish? Any signs of manifestation?

____

Small Wins:

____

CHAPTER XXXVI

Day 36

"The best preparation for tomorrow is doing your best today." — H. Jackson Brown, Jr.

Morning Affirmations

Write 5 affirmations as you start the day. (A few suggestions for affirmations as below)

"I am worthy of success and abundance."
"I trust in the process of life."
"I release all fear and embrace confidence."

1. ____
2. ____
3. ____
4. ____
5. ____

Visualization & Intention Setting

Spend 5-10 minutes visualizing yourself as the confident, successful, abundant person you're becoming.

Today's Intentions:

1. ____
2. ____
3. ____

Gratitude Practice

List 3 things you're grateful for today:

1. ____
2. ____
3. ____

Daily Action Towards Goals

What is one action you can take today that aligns with your goals?

____

Evening Reflection & Acknowledgment

How did you feel today? What did you accomplish? Any signs of manifestation?

____

Small Wins:

____

CHAPTER XXXVII

Day 37

"The best revenge is massive success." — Frank Sinatra

Morning Affirmations

Write 5 affirmations as you start the day. (A few suggestions for affirmations as below)

"I am worthy of success and abundance."
"I trust in the process of life."
"I release all fear and embrace confidence."

1. ____
2. ____
3. ____
4. ____
5. ____

Visualization & Intention Setting

Spend 5-10 minutes visualizing yourself as the confident, successful, abundant person you're becoming.

Today's Intentions:

1. ____
2. ____
3. ____

Gratitude Practice

List 3 things you're grateful for today:

1. ____
2. ____
3. ____

Daily Action Towards Goals

What is one action you can take today that aligns with your goals?

____

Evening Reflection & Acknowledgment

How did you feel today? What did you accomplish? Any signs of manifestation?

____

Small Wins:

____

CHAPTER XXXVIII

Day 38

"The quieter you become, the more you can hear."
— Ram Dass

Morning Affirmations

Write 5 affirmations as you start the day. (A few suggestions for affirmations as below)

"I am worthy of success and abundance."
"I trust in the process of life."
"I release all fear and embrace confidence."

1. ____
2. ____
3. ____
4. ____
5. ____

Visualization & Intention Setting

Spend 5-10 minutes visualizing yourself as the confident, successful, abundant person you're becoming.

Today's Intentions:

1. ____
2. ____
3. ____

Gratitude Practice

List 3 things you're grateful for today:

1. ____
2. ____
3. ____

Daily Action Towards Goals

What is one action you can take today that aligns with your goals?

____

Evening Reflection & Acknowledgment

How did you feel today? What did you accomplish? Any signs of manifestation?

____

Small Wins:

____

CHAPTER XXXIX

Day 39

"When something is important enough, you do it even if the odds are not in your favor." – Elon Musk

Morning Affirmations

Write 5 affirmations as you start the day. (A few suggestions for affirmations as below)

"I am worthy of success and abundance."
"I trust in the process of life."
"I release all fear and embrace confidence."

1. ____
2. ____
3. ____
4. ____
5. ____

Visualization & Intention Setting

Spend 5-10 minutes visualizing yourself as the confident, successful, abundant person you're becoming.

Today's Intentions:

1. ____
2. ____
3. ____

Gratitude Practice

List 3 things you're grateful for today:

    1. _______________________________________

    2. _______________________________________

    3. _______________________________________

Daily Action Towards Goals

What is one action you can take today that aligns with your goals?

____

Evening Reflection & Acknowledgment

How did you feel today? What did you accomplish? Any signs of manifestation?

____

Small Wins:

____

CHAPTER XL

Day 40

"Keep your face always toward the sunshine, and shadows will fall behind you." – Walt Whitman

Morning Affirmations

Write 5 affirmations as you start the day. (A few suggestions for affirmations as below)

"I am worthy of success and abundance."
"I trust in the process of life."
"I release all fear and embrace confidence."

1. ____
2. ____
3. ____
4. ____
5. ____

Visualization & Intention Setting

Spend 5-10 minutes visualizing yourself as the confident, successful, abundant person you're becoming.

Today's Intentions:

1. ____
2. ____
3. ____

Gratitude Practice

List 3 things you're grateful for today:

1. ____
2. ____
3. ____

Daily Action Towards Goals

What is one action you can take today that aligns with your goals?
____

Evening Reflection & Acknowledgment

How did you feel today? What did you accomplish? Any signs of manifestation?
____

Small Wins:
____

CHAPTER XLI

Day 41

"The bad news is time flies. The good news is you're the pilot." – Michael Altshuler

Morning Affirmations

Write 5 affirmations as you start the day. (A few suggestions for affirmations as below)

"I am worthy of success and abundance."
"I trust in the process of life."
"I release all fear and embrace confidence."

1. _______________________________________
2. _______________________________________
3. _______________________________________
4. _______________________________________
5. _______________________________________

Visualization & Intention Setting

Spend 5-10 minutes visualizing yourself as the confident, successful, abundant person you're becoming.

Today's Intentions:

1. _______________________________________
2. _______________________________________
3. _______________________________________

Gratitude Practice

List 3 things you're grateful for today:

1. _______________________________________
2. _______________________________________
3. _______________________________________

Daily Action Towards Goals

What is one action you can take today that aligns with your goals?

____

Evening Reflection & Acknowledgment

How did you feel today? What did you accomplish? Any signs of manifestation?

____

Small Wins:

____

CHAPTER XLII

Day 42

""You were born to win, but to be a winner, you must plan to win, prepare to win, and expect to win." Zig Ziglar"

Morning Affirmations

Write 5 affirmations as you start the day. (A few suggestions for affirmations as below)
"I am worthy of success and abundance."
"I trust in the process of life."
"I release all fear and embrace confidence."

1. ____
2. ____
3. ____
4. ____
5. ____

Visualization & Intention Setting

Spend 5-10 minutes visualizing yourself as the confident, successful, abundant person you're becoming.
Today's Intentions:

1. ____
2. ____
3. ____

Gratitude Practice

List 3 things you're grateful for today:

1. ____
2. ____

3. _______________________________________

Daily Action Towards Goals

What is one action you can take today that aligns with your goals?

____

Evening Reflection & Acknowledgment

How did you feel today? What did you accomplish? Any signs of manifestation?

____

Small Wins:

____

CHAPTER XLIII

Day 43

"I can't change the direction of the wind, but I can adjust my sails to always reach my destination." – Jimmy Dean

Morning Affirmations

Write 5 affirmations as you start the day. (A few suggestions for affirmations as below)

"I am worthy of success and abundance."
"I trust in the process of life."
"I release all fear and embrace confidence."

1. ____
2. ____
3. ____
4. ____
5. ____

Visualization & Intention Setting

Spend 5-10 minutes visualizing yourself as the confident, successful, abundant person you're becoming.

Today's Intentions:

1. ____
2. ____
3. ____

Gratitude Practice

List 3 things you're grateful for today:

1. ____
2. ____
3. ____

Daily Action Towards Goals

What is one action you can take today that aligns with your goals?

____

Evening Reflection & Acknowledgment

How did you feel today? What did you accomplish? Any signs of manifestation?

____

Small Wins:

____

CHAPTER XLIV

Day 44

"There are no limits to what you can accomplish, except the limits you place on your own thinking."
– Brian Tracy

Morning Affirmations

Write 5 affirmations as you start the day. (A few suggestions for affirmations as below)

"I am worthy of success and abundance."
"I trust in the process of life."
"I release all fear and embrace confidence."

1. ____
2. ____
3. ____
4. ____
5. ____

Visualization & Intention Setting

Spend 5-10 minutes visualizing yourself as the confident, successful, abundant person you're becoming.

Today's Intentions:

1. ____
2. ____
3. ____

Gratitude Practice

List 3 things you're grateful for today:

1. ____
2. ____
3. ____

Daily Action Towards Goals

What is one action you can take today that aligns with your goals?

____

Evening Reflection & Acknowledgment

How did you feel today? What did you accomplish? Any signs of manifestation?

____

Small Wins:

____

CHAPTER XLV

Day 45

"The greatest weapon against stress is our ability to choose one thought over another."— William James

Morning Affirmations

Write 5 affirmations as you start the day. (A few suggestions for affirmations as below)

"I am worthy of success and abundance."
"I trust in the process of life."
"I release all fear and embrace confidence."

1. ______________________________________
2. ______________________________________
3. ______________________________________
4. ______________________________________
5. ______________________________________

Visualization & Intention Setting

Spend 5-10 minutes visualizing yourself as the confident, successful, abundant person you're becoming.

Today's Intentions:

1. ______________________________________
2. ______________________________________
3. ______________________________________

Gratitude Practice

List 3 things you're grateful for today:

1. ____
2. ____
3. ____

Daily Action Towards Goals

What is one action you can take today that aligns with your goals?

____

Evening Reflection & Acknowledgment

How did you feel today? What did you accomplish? Any signs of manifestation?

____

Small Wins:

____

CHAPTER XLVI

Day 46

"Doing the best at this moment puts you in the best place for the next moment." — Oprah Winfrey

Morning Affirmations

Write 5 affirmations as you start the day. (A few suggestions for affirmations as below)

"I am worthy of success and abundance."
"I trust in the process of life."
"I release all fear and embrace confidence."

1. ____
2. ____
3. ____
4. ____
5. ____

Visualization & Intention Setting

Spend 5-10 minutes visualizing yourself as the confident, successful, abundant person you're becoming.

Today's Intentions:

1. ____
2. ____
3. ____

Gratitude Practice

List 3 things you're grateful for today:

1. ____
2. ____
3. ____

Daily Action Towards Goals

What is one action you can take today that aligns with your goals?

____

Evening Reflection & Acknowledgment

How did you feel today? What did you accomplish? Any signs of manifestation?

____

Small Wins:

____

CHAPTER XLVII

Day 47

"Life is like riding a bicycle. To keep your balance, you must keep moving."— Albert Einstein

Morning Affirmations

Write 5 affirmations as you start the day. (A few suggestions for affirmations as below)

"I am worthy of success and abundance."
"I trust in the process of life."
"I release all fear and embrace confidence."

1. ____
2. ____
3. ____
4. ____
5. ____

Visualization & Intention Setting

Spend 5-10 minutes visualizing yourself as the confident, successful, abundant person you're becoming.

Today's Intentions:

1. ____
2. ____
3. ____

Gratitude Practice

List 3 things you're grateful for today:

1. _______________________________________
2. _______________________________________
3. _______________________________________

Daily Action Towards Goals

What is one action you can take today that aligns with your goals?

____

Evening Reflection & Acknowledgment

How did you feel today? What did you accomplish? Any signs of manifestation?

____

Small Wins:

____

CHAPTER XLVIII

Day 48

You experience external change only once you change internally. Start today and watch how everything around you begins to change! - Unknown

Morning Affirmations

Write 5 affirmations as you start the day. (A few suggestions for affirmations as below)

"I am worthy of success and abundance."
"I trust in the process of life."
"I release all fear and embrace confidence."

1. ____
2. ____
3. ____
4. ____
5. ____

Visualization & Intention Setting

Spend 5-10 minutes visualizing yourself as the confident, successful, abundant person you're becoming.

Today's Intentions:

1. ____
2. ____
3. ____

Gratitude Practice

List 3 things you're grateful for today:

1. ____
2. ____
3. ____

Daily Action Towards Goals

What is one action you can take today that aligns with your goals?

____

Evening Reflection & Acknowledgment

How did you feel today? What did you accomplish? Any signs of manifestation?

____

Small Wins:

____

CHAPTER XLIX

Day 49

"Optimism is the one quality more associated with success and happiness than any other."- Brian Tracy

Morning Affirmations

Write 5 affirmations as you start the day. (A few suggestions for affirmations as below)

"I am worthy of success and abundance."
"I trust in the process of life."
"I release all fear and embrace confidence."

1. ____
2. ____
3. ____
4. ____
5. ____

Visualization & Intention Setting

Spend 5-10 minutes visualizing yourself as the confident, successful, abundant person you're becoming.

Today's Intentions:

1. ____
2. ____
3. ____

Gratitude Practice

List 3 things you're grateful for today:

1. ____
2. ____
3. ____

Daily Action Towards Goals

What is one action you can take today that aligns with your goals?

____

Evening Reflection & Acknowledgment

How did you feel today? What did you accomplish? Any signs of manifestation?

____

Small Wins:

____

CHAPTER L

Day 50

"Go as far as you can see; when you get there, you'll be able to see further." —Thomas Carlyle

Morning Affirmations

Write 5 affirmations as you start the day. (A few suggestions for affirmations as below)

"I am worthy of success and abundance."
"I trust in the process of life."
"I release all fear and embrace confidence."

1. ____
2. ____
3. ____
4. ____
5. ____

Visualization & Intention Setting

Spend 5-10 minutes visualizing yourself as the confident, successful, abundant person you're becoming.

Today's Intentions:

1. ____
2. ____
3. ____

Gratitude Practice

List 3 things you're grateful for today:

1. ____
2. ____
3. ____

Daily Action Towards Goals

What is one action you can take today that aligns with your goals?

____

Evening Reflection & Acknowledgment

How did you feel today? What did you accomplish? Any signs of manifestation?

____

Small Wins:

____

CHAPTER LI

Day 51

"If you don't like the road you're walking, start paving another one." – Dolly Parton

Morning Affirmations

Write 5 affirmations as you start the day. (A few suggestions for affirmations as below)

"I am worthy of success and abundance."
"I trust in the process of life."
"I release all fear and embrace confidence."

1. ____
2. ____
3. ____
4. ____
5. ____

Visualization & Intention Setting

Spend 5-10 minutes visualizing yourself as the confident, successful, abundant person you're becoming.

Today's Intentions:

1. ____
2. ____
3. ____

Gratitude Practice

List 3 things you're grateful for today:

1. ______________________________________
2. ______________________________________
3. ______________________________________

Daily Action Towards Goals

What is one action you can take today that aligns with your goals?

____

Evening Reflection & Acknowledgment

How did you feel today? What did you accomplish? Any signs of manifestation?

____

Small Wins:

____

CHAPTER LII

Day 52

"Happiness is not by chance, but by choice." – Jim Rohn

Morning Affirmations

Write 5 affirmations as you start the day. (A few suggestions for affirmations as below)

"I am worthy of success and abundance."
"I trust in the process of life."
"I release all fear and embrace confidence."

1. ____
2. ____
3. ____
4. ____
5. ____

Visualization & Intention Setting

Spend 5-10 minutes visualizing yourself as the confident, successful, abundant person you're becoming.

Today's Intentions:

1. ____
2. ____
3. ____

Gratitude Practice

List 3 things you're grateful for today:

1. _______________________________________
2. _______________________________________
3. _______________________________________

Daily Action Towards Goals

What is one action you can take today that aligns with your goals?

____

Evening Reflection & Acknowledgment

How did you feel today? What did you accomplish? Any signs of manifestation?

____

Small Wins:

____

CHAPTER LIII

Day 53

"People who are crazy enough to think they can change the world, are the ones who do."- Rob Siltanen

Morning Affirmations

Write 5 affirmations as you start the day. (A few suggestions for affirmations as below)

"I am worthy of success and abundance."
"I trust in the process of life."
"I release all fear and embrace confidence."

1. ____
2. ____
3. ____
4. ____
5. ____

Visualization & Intention Setting

Spend 5-10 minutes visualizing yourself as the confident, successful, abundant person you're becoming.

Today's Intentions:

1. ____
2. ____
3. ____

Gratitude Practice

List 3 things you're grateful for today:

1. ____
2. ____
3. ____

Daily Action Towards Goals

What is one action you can take today that aligns with your goals?

____

Evening Reflection & Acknowledgment

How did you feel today? What did you accomplish? Any signs of manifestation?

____

Small Wins:

____

Day 54

"My best friend is the one who brings out the best in me." — Henry Ford

Morning Affirmations

Write 5 affirmations as you start the day. (A few suggestions for affirmations as below)

"I am worthy of success and abundance."
"I trust in the process of life."
"I release all fear and embrace confidence."

1. ____
2. ____
3. ____
4. ____
5. ____

Visualization & Intention Setting

Spend 5-10 minutes visualizing yourself as the confident, successful, abundant person you're becoming.

Today's Intentions:

1. ____
2. ____
3. ____

Gratitude Practice

List 3 things you're grateful for today:

1. _______________________________________
2. _______________________________________
3. _______________________________________

Daily Action Towards Goals

What is one action you can take today that aligns with your goals?

____

Evening Reflection & Acknowledgment

How did you feel today? What did you accomplish? Any signs of manifestation?

____

Small Wins:

____

CHAPTER LV

Day 55

"If I cannot do great things, I can do small things in a great way." – Martin Luther King, Jr

Morning Affirmations

Write 5 affirmations as you start the day. (A few suggestions for affirmations as below)

"I am worthy of success and abundance."
"I trust in the process of life."
"I release all fear and embrace confidence."

1. ____
2. ____
3. ____
4. ____
5. ____

Visualization & Intention Setting

Spend 5-10 minutes visualizing yourself as the confident, successful, abundant person you're becoming.

Today's Intentions:

1. ____
2. ____
3. ____

Gratitude Practice

List 3 things you're grateful for today:

1. ____
2. ____
3. ____

Daily Action Towards Goals

What is one action you can take today that aligns with your goals?

____

Evening Reflection & Acknowledgment

How did you feel today? What did you accomplish? Any signs of manifestation?

____

Small Wins:

____

CHAPTER LVI

Day 56

"A genius is often merely a talented person who has done all of his or her homework." – Thomas Edison

Morning Affirmations

Write 5 affirmations as you start the day. (A few suggestions for affirmations as below)

"I am worthy of success and abundance."
"I trust in the process of life."
"I release all fear and embrace confidence."

1. ____
2. ____
3. ____
4. ____
5. ____

Visualization & Intention Setting

Spend 5-10 minutes visualizing yourself as the confident, successful, abundant person you're becoming.

Today's Intentions:

1. ____
2. ____
3. ____

Gratitude Practice

List 3 things you're grateful for today:

1. ____
2. ____
3. ____

Daily Action Towards Goals

What is one action you can take today that aligns with your goals?

____

Evening Reflection & Acknowledgment

How did you feel today? What did you accomplish? Any signs of manifestation?

____

Small Wins:

____

CHAPTER LVII

Day 57

"You can't cross the sea merely by standing and staring at the water." — Rabindranath Tagore

Morning Affirmations

Write 5 affirmations as you start the day. (A few suggestions for affirmations as below)

"I am worthy of success and abundance."
"I trust in the process of life."
"I release all fear and embrace confidence."

1. ____
2. ____
3. ____
4. ____
5. ____

Visualization & Intention Setting

Spend 5-10 minutes visualizing yourself as the confident, successful, abundant person you're becoming.

.Today's Intentions:

1. ____
2. ____
3. ____

Gratitude Practice

List 3 things you're grateful for today:

1. ____
2. ____
3. ____

Daily Action Towards Goals

What is one action you can take today that aligns with your goals?

____

Evening Reflection & Acknowledgment

How did you feel today? What did you accomplish? Any signs of manifestation?

____

Small Wins:

____

CHAPTER LVIII

Day 58

"Don't stop when you're tired, stop when you're done." — David Goggins

Morning Affirmations

Write 5 affirmations as you start the day. (A few suggestions for affirmations as below)

"I am worthy of success and abundance."
"I trust in the process of life."
"I release all fear and embrace confidence."

1. ____
2. ____
3. ____
4. ____
5. ____

Visualization & Intention Setting

Spend 5-10 minutes visualizing yourself as the confident, successful, abundant person you're becoming.

Today's Intentions:

1. ____
2. ____
3. ____

Gratitude Practice

List 3 things you're grateful for today:

1. _______________________________________
2. _______________________________________
3. _______________________________________

Daily Action Towards Goals

What is one action you can take today that aligns with your goals?

____

Evening Reflection & Acknowledgment

How did you feel today? What did you accomplish? Any signs of manifestation?

____

Small Wins:

____

CHAPTER LIX

Day 59

"You don't always need a plan. Sometimes you just need to breathe, trust, let go and see what happens." — Mandy Hale

Morning Affirmations

Write 5 affirmations as you start the day. (A few suggestions for affirmations as below)

"I am worthy of success and abundance."
"I trust in the process of life."
"I release all fear and embrace confidence."

1. ______________________________________
2. ______________________________________
3. ______________________________________
4. ______________________________________
5. ______________________________________

Visualization & Intention Setting

Spend 5-10 minutes visualizing yourself as the confident, successful, abundant person you're becoming.

Today's Intentions:

1. ______________________________________
2. ______________________________________
3. ______________________________________

Gratitude Practice

List 3 things you're grateful for today:

1. ____
2. ____
3. ____

Daily Action Towards Goals

What is one action you can take today that aligns with your goals?

____

Evening Reflection & Acknowledgment

How did you feel today? What did you accomplish? Any signs of manifestation?

____

Small Wins:

____

CHAPTER LX

Day 60

"Belief creates the actual fact." — William James

Morning Affirmations

Write 5 affirmations as you start the day. (A few suggestions for affirmations as below)

"I am worthy of success and abundance."
"I trust in the process of life."
"I release all fear and embrace confidence."

1. ____
2. ____
3. ____
4. ____
5. ____

Visualization & Intention Setting

Spend 5-10 minutes visualizing yourself as the confident, successful, abundant person you're becoming.

Today's Intentions:

1. ____
2. ____
3. ____

Gratitude Practice

List 3 things you're grateful for today:

1. ____

2. _______________________________________

3. _______________________________________

Daily Action Towards Goals

What is one action you can take today that aligns with your goals?

____

Evening Reflection & Acknowledgment

How did you feel today? What did you accomplish? Any signs of manifestation?

____

Small Wins:

____

CHAPTER LXI

Day 61

"Weaknesses are just strengths in the wrong environment." — Marianne Cantwell

Morning Affirmations

Write 5 affirmations as you start the day. (A few suggestions for affirmations as below)

"I am worthy of success and abundance."
"I trust in the process of life."
"I release all fear and embrace confidence."

1. ____
2. ____
3. ____
4. ____
5. ____

Visualization & Intention Setting

Spend 5-10 minutes visualizing yourself as the confident, successful, abundant person you're becoming.

Today's Intentions:

1. ____
2. ____
3. ____

Gratitude Practice

List 3 things you're grateful for today:

1. ____
2. ____
3. ____

Daily Action Towards Goals

What is one action you can take today that aligns with your goals?

____

Evening Reflection & Acknowledgment

How did you feel today? What did you accomplish? Any signs of manifestation?

____

Small Wins:

____

CHAPTER LXII

Day 62

"When it comes to luck, you make your own." — **Bruce Springsteen**

Morning Affirmations

Write 5 affirmations as you start the day. (A few suggestions for affirmations as below)

"I am worthy of success and abundance."
"I trust in the process of life."
"I release all fear and embrace confidence."

1. ____
2. ____
3. ____
4. ____
5. ____

Visualization & Intention Setting

Spend 5-10 minutes visualizing yourself as the confident, successful, abundant person you're becoming.

Today's Intentions:

1. ____
2. ____
3. ____

Gratitude Practice

List 3 things you're grateful for today:

1. ____
2. ____
3. ____

Daily Action Towards Goals

What is one action you can take today that aligns with your goals?

____

Evening Reflection & Acknowledgment

How did you feel today? What did you accomplish? Any signs of manifestation?

____

Small Wins:

____

CHAPTER LXIII

Day 63

"You have to be where you are to get where you need to go." — Amy Poehler

Morning Affirmations

Write 5 affirmations as you start the day. (A few suggestions for affirmations as below)
"I am worthy of success and abundance."
"I trust in the process of life."
"I release all fear and embrace confidence."
1. ____
2. ____
3. ____
4. ____
5. ____

Visualization & Intention Setting

Spend 5-10 minutes visualizing yourself as the confident, successful, abundant person you're becoming.
Today's Intentions:
1. ____
2. ____
3. ____

Gratitude Practice

List 3 things you're grateful for today:

1. ____
2. ____
3. ____

Daily Action Towards Goals

What is one action you can take today that aligns with your goals?

____

Evening Reflection & Acknowledgment

How did you feel today? What did you accomplish? Any signs of manifestation?

____

Small Wins:

____

CHAPTER LXIV

Day 64

"It is in your moments of decision that your destiny is shaped." — Tony Robbins

Morning Affirmations

Write 5 affirmations as you start the day. (A few suggestions for affirmations as below)

"I am worthy of success and abundance."
"I trust in the process of life."
"I release all fear and embrace confidence."

1. ____
2. ____
3. ____
4. ____
5. ____

Visualization & Intention Setting

Spend 5-10 minutes visualizing yourself as the confident, successful, abundant person you're becoming.

Today's Intentions:
1. ____
2. ____
3. ____

Gratitude Practice

List 3 things you're grateful for today:

1. ____
2. ____
3. ____

Daily Action Towards Goals

What is one action you can take today that aligns with your goals?

____

Evening Reflection & Acknowledgment

How did you feel today? What did you accomplish? Any signs of manifestation?

____

Small Wins:

____

CHAPTER LXV

Day 65

"Your talent is God's gift to you. What you do with it is your gift back to God." — Leo Buscaglia

Morning Affirmations

Write 5 affirmations as you start the day. (A few suggestions for affirmations as below)

"I am worthy of success and abundance."
"I trust in the process of life."
"I release all fear and embrace confidence."

1. ____
2. ____
3. ____
4. ____
5. ____

Visualization & Intention Setting

Spend 5-10 minutes visualizing yourself as the confident, successful, abundant person you're becoming.

Today's Intentions:

1. ____
2. ____
3. ____

Gratitude Practice

List 3 things you're grateful for today:

1. ____
2. ____
3. ____

Daily Action Towards Goals

What is one action you can take today that aligns with your goals?

____

Evening Reflection & Acknowledgment

How did you feel today? What did you accomplish? Any signs of manifestation?

____

Small Wins:

____

Day 66

"Opportunity does not knock; it presents itself when you beat down the door." — Kyle Chandler

Morning Affirmations

Write 5 affirmations as you start the day. (A few suggestions for affirmations as below)

"I am worthy of success and abundance."
"I trust in the process of life."
"I release all fear and embrace confidence."

1. ___________________________________
2. ___________________________________
3. ___________________________________
4. ___________________________________
5. ___________________________________

Visualization & Intention Setting

Spend 5-10 minutes visualizing yourself as the confident, successful, abundant person you're becoming.

Today's Intentions:

1. ___________________________________
2. ___________________________________
3. ___________________________________

Gratitude Practice

List 3 things you're grateful for today:

1. ____
2. ____
3. ____

Daily Action Towards Goals

What is one action you can take today that aligns with your goals?

____

Evening Reflection & Acknowledgment

How did you feel today? What did you accomplish? Any signs of manifestation?

____

Small Wins:

____

CHAPTER LXVII

Day 67

"What you do today can improve all your tomorrows." — Ralph Marston

Morning Affirmations

Write 5 affirmations as you start the day. (A few suggestions for affirmations as below)

"I am worthy of success and abundance."
"I trust in the process of life."
"I release all fear and embrace confidence."

1. ____
2. ____
3. ____
4. ____
5. ____

Visualization & Intention Setting

Spend 5-10 minutes visualizing yourself as the confident, successful, abundant person you're becoming.

Today's Intentions:

1. ____
2. ____
3. ____

Gratitude Practice

List 3 things you're grateful for today:

1. _______________________________________
2. _______________________________________
3. _______________________________________

Daily Action Towards Goals

What is one action you can take today that aligns with your goals?

____

Evening Reflection & Acknowledgment

How did you feel today? What did you accomplish? Any signs of manifestation?

____

Small Wins:

____

CHAPTER LXVIII

Day 68

"If people are doubting how far you can go, go so far that you can't hear them anymore." —Michele Ruiz

Morning Affirmations

Write 5 affirmations as you start the day. (A few suggestions for affirmations as below)

"I am worthy of success and abundance."
"I trust in the process of life."
"I release all fear and embrace confidence."

1. _______________________________________
2. _______________________________________
3. _______________________________________
4. _______________________________________
5. _______________________________________

Visualization & Intention Setting

Spend 5-10 minutes visualizing yourself as the confident, successful, abundant person you're becoming.

Today's Intentions:

1. _______________________________________
2. _______________________________________
3. _______________________________________

Gratitude Practice

List 3 things you're grateful for today:

1. ____
2. ____
3. ____

Daily Action Towards Goals

What is one action you can take today that aligns with your goals?

____

Evening Reflection & Acknowledgment

How did you feel today? What did you accomplish? Any signs of manifestation?

____

Small Wins:

____

CHAPTER LXIX

Day 69

"Hustle in silence and let your success make the noise." —Unknown

Morning Affirmations

Write 5 affirmations as you start the day. (A few suggestions for affirmations as below)

"I am worthy of success and abundance."
"I trust in the process of life."
"I release all fear and embrace confidence."

1. _______________________________________
2. _______________________________________
3. _______________________________________
4. _______________________________________
5. _______________________________________

Visualization & Intention Setting

Spend 5-10 minutes visualizing yourself as the confident, successful, abundant person you're becoming.

Today's Intentions:

1. _______________________________________
2. _______________________________________
3. _______________________________________

Gratitude Practice

List 3 things you're grateful for today:

1. ____
2. ____
3. ____

Daily Action Towards Goals

What is one action you can take today that aligns with your goals?

____

Evening Reflection & Acknowledgment

How did you feel today? What did you accomplish? Any signs of manifestation?

____

Small Wins:

____

CHAPTER LXX

Day 70

"The hard days are what make you stronger."
—Aly Raisman

Morning Affirmations

Write 5 affirmations as you start the day. (A few suggestions for affirmations as below)

"I am worthy of success and abundance."
"I trust in the process of life."
"I release all fear and embrace confidence."

1. ____
2. ____
3. ____
4. ____
5. ____

Visualization & Intention Setting

Spend 5-10 minutes visualizing yourself as the confident, successful, abundant person you're becoming.

Today's Intentions:

1. ____
2. ____
3. ____

Gratitude Practice

List 3 things you're grateful for today:

1. _______________________________________
2. _______________________________________
3. _______________________________________

Daily Action Towards Goals

What is one action you can take today that aligns with your goals?

____

Evening Reflection & Acknowledgment

How did you feel today? What did you accomplish? Any signs of manifestation?

____

Small Wins:

____

CHAPTER LXXI

Day 71

"You don't need to see the whole staircase, just take the first step." —*Martin Luther King Jr.*

Morning Affirmations

Write 5 affirmations as you start the day. (A few suggestions for affirmations as below)

"I am worthy of success and abundance."
"I trust in the process of life."
"I release all fear and embrace confidence."

1. ____
2. ____
3. ____
4. ____
5. ____

Visualization & Intention Setting

Spend 5-10 minutes visualizing yourself as the confident, successful, abundant person you're becoming.

Today's Intentions:

1. ____
2. ____
3. ____

Gratitude Practice

List 3 things you're grateful for today:

1. ____
2. ____
3. ____

Daily Action Towards Goals

What is one action you can take today that aligns with your goals?

____

Evening Reflection & Acknowledgment

How did you feel today? What did you accomplish? Any signs of manifestation?

____

Small Wins:

____

CHAPTER LXXII

Day 72

"You never know what you can do until you try."
—William Cobbett

Morning Affirmations

Write 5 affirmations as you start the day. (A few suggestions for affirmations as below)

"I am worthy of success and abundance."
"I trust in the process of life."
"I release all fear and embrace confidence."

   1. ____
   2. ____
   3. ____
   4. ____
   5. ____

Visualization & Intention Setting

Spend 5-10 minutes visualizing yourself as the confident, successful, abundant person you're becoming.

   Today's Intentions:
   1. ____
   2. ____
   3. ____

Gratitude Practice

List 3 things you're grateful for today:

1. ____
2. ____
3. ____

Daily Action Towards Goals

What is one action you can take today that aligns with your goals?

____

Evening Reflection & Acknowledgment

How did you feel today? What did you accomplish? Any signs of manifestation?

____

Small Wins:

____

CHAPTER LXXIII

Day 73

"Action is the foundational key to all success."
—Pablo Picasso

Morning Affirmations

Write 5 affirmations as you start the day. (A few suggestions for affirmations as below)

"I am worthy of success and abundance."
"I trust in the process of life."
"I release all fear and embrace confidence."

1. ____
2. ____
3. ____
4. ____
5. ____

Visualization & Intention Setting

Spend 5-10 minutes visualizing yourself as the confident, successful, abundant person you're becoming.

Today's Intentions:

1. ____
2. ____
3. ____

Gratitude Practice

List 3 things you're grateful for today:

1. ____
2. ____
3. ____

Daily Action Towards Goals

What is one action you can take today that aligns with your goals?

____

Evening Reflection & Acknowledgment

How did you feel today? What did you accomplish? Any signs of manifestation?

____

Small Wins:

____

CHAPTER LXXIV

Day 74

*"The secret of change is to focus all your energy,
not on fighting the old, but on building the new."*
—Socrates

Morning Affirmations

Write 5 affirmations as you start the day. (A few suggestions for affirmations as below)

"I am worthy of success and abundance."
"I trust in the process of life."
"I release all fear and embrace confidence."

1. ____
2. ____
3. ____
4. ____
5. ____

Visualization & Intention Setting

Spend 5-10 minutes visualizing yourself as the confident, successful, abundant person you're becoming.

Today's Intentions:

1. ____
2. ____
3. ____

Gratitude Practice

List 3 things you're grateful for today:

1. ____
2. ____
3. ____

Daily Action Towards Goals

What is one action you can take today that aligns with your goals?

____

Evening Reflection & Acknowledgment

How did you feel today? What did you accomplish? Any signs of manifestation?

____

Small Wins:

____

CHAPTER LXXV

Day 75

"It is impossible to live without failing at something, unless you live so cautiously that you might as well not have lived at all—in which case, you fail by default." —J.K. Rowling

Morning Affirmations

Write 5 affirmations as you start the day. (A few suggestions for affirmations as below)

"I am worthy of success and abundance."
"I trust in the process of life."
"I release all fear and embrace confidence."

1. ____
2. ____
3. ____
4. ____
5. ____

Visualization & Intention Setting

Spend 5-10 minutes visualizing yourself as the confident, successful, abundant person you're becoming.

Today's Intentions:

1. ____
2. ____
3. ____

Gratitude Practice

List 3 things you're grateful for today:

1. ____
2. ____
3. ____

Daily Action Towards Goals

What is one action you can take today that aligns with your goals?

____

Evening Reflection & Acknowledgment

How did you feel today? What did you accomplish? Any signs of manifestation?

____

Small Wins:

____

CHAPTER LXXVI

Day 76

"If you get tired, learn to rest, not to quit." – Banksy

Morning Affirmations

Write 5 affirmations as you start the day. (A few suggestions for affirmations as below)

"I am worthy of success and abundance."
"I trust in the process of life."
"I release all fear and embrace confidence."

1. ____
2. ____
3. ____
4. ____
5. ____

Visualization & Intention Setting

Spend 5-10 minutes visualizing yourself as the confident, successful, abundant person you're becoming.

Today's Intentions:

1. ____
2. ____
3. ____

Gratitude Practice

List 3 things you're grateful for today:

1. _______________________________________
2. _______________________________________
3. _______________________________________

Daily Action Towards Goals

What is one action you can take today that aligns with your goals?

____

Evening Reflection & Acknowledgment

How did you feel today? What did you accomplish? Any signs of manifestation?

____

Small Wins:

____

CHAPTER LXXVII

Day 77

"Be the best of whatever you are." — *Martin Luther King, Jr.*

Morning Affirmations

Write 5 affirmations as you start the day. (A few suggestions for affirmations as below)

"I am worthy of success and abundance."
"I trust in the process of life."
"I release all fear and embrace confidence."

1. ____
2. ____
3. ____
4. ____
5. ____

Visualization & Intention Setting

Spend 5-10 minutes visualizing yourself as the confident, successful, abundant person you're becoming.

Today's Intentions:

1. ____
2. ____
3. ____

Gratitude Practice

List 3 things you're grateful for today:

1. ____
2. ____
3. ____

Daily Action Towards Goals

What is one action you can take today that aligns with your goals?

____

Evening Reflection & Acknowledgment

How did you feel today? What did you accomplish? Any signs of manifestation?

____

Small Wins:

____

CHAPTER LXXVIII

Day 78

Courage doesn't always roar. Sometimes courage is the quiet voice at the end of the day saying, "I will try again tomorrow." – Mary Anne Radmacher

Morning Affirmations

Write 5 affirmations as you start the day. (A few suggestions for affirmations as below)

"I am worthy of success and abundance."

"I trust in the process of life."

"I release all fear and embrace confidence."

1. ____
2. ____
3. ____
4. ____
5. ____

Visualization & Intention Setting

Spend 5-10 minutes visualizing yourself as the confident, successful, abundant person you're becoming.

Today's Intentions:

1. ____
2. ____
3. ____

Gratitude Practice

List 3 things you're grateful for today:
  1. ____
  2. ____
  3. ____

Daily Action Towards Goals

What is one action you can take today that aligns with your goals?

____

Evening Reflection & Acknowledgment

How did you feel today? What did you accomplish? Any signs of manifestation?

____

Small Wins:

____

Day 79

"You can't go back and change the beginning, but you can start where you are and change the ending." – C.S. Lewis

Morning Affirmations

Write 5 affirmations as you start the day. (A few suggestions for affirmations as below)

"I am worthy of success and abundance."
"I trust in the process of life."
"I release all fear and embrace confidence."

1. ____
2. ____
3. ____
4. ____
5. ____

Visualization & Intention Setting

Spend 5-10 minutes visualizing yourself as the confident, successful, abundant person you're becoming.

Today's Intentions:

1. ____
2. ____
3. ____

Gratitude Practice

List 3 things you're grateful for today:

1. ____
2. ____
3. ____

Daily Action Towards Goals

What is one action you can take today that aligns with your goals?

____

Evening Reflection & Acknowledgment

How did you feel today? What did you accomplish? Any signs of manifestation?

____

Small Wins:

____

CHAPTER LXXX

Day 80

"When you focus on the good, the good gets better." – Abraham Hicks

Morning Affirmations

Write 5 affirmations as you start the day. (A few suggestions for affirmations as below)

"I am worthy of success and abundance."
"I trust in the process of life."
"I release all fear and embrace confidence."

1. ____
2. ____
3. ____
4. ____
5. ____

Visualization & Intention Setting

Spend 5-10 minutes visualizing yourself as the confident, successful, abundant person you're becoming.

Today's Intentions:

1. ____
2. ____
3. ____

Gratitude Practice

List 3 things you're grateful for today:

1. ____
2. ____
3. ____

Daily Action Towards Goals

What is one action you can take today that aligns with your goals?

____

Evening Reflection & Acknowledgment

How did you feel today? What did you accomplish? Any signs of manifestation?

____

Small Wins:

____

Day 81

"Failure is not the opposite of success; it's part of success." – Arianna Huffington

Day 82

"If you want to live a happy life, tie it to a goal, not to people or things." – Albert Einstein

Morning Affirmations

Write 5 affirmations as you start the day. (A few suggestions for affirmations as below)

"I am worthy of success and abundance."
"I trust in the process of life."
"I release all fear and embrace confidence."

1. ____
2. ____
3. ____
4. ____
5. ____

Visualization & Intention Setting

Spend 5-10 minutes visualizing yourself as the confident, successful, abundant person you're becoming.

Today's Intentions:

1. ____
2. ____
3. ____

Gratitude Practice

List 3 things you're grateful for today:

1. ______________________________
2. ______________________________
3. ______________________________

Daily Action Towards Goals

What is one action you can take today that aligns with your goals?

____

Evening Reflection & Acknowledgment

How did you feel today? What did you accomplish? Any signs of manifestation?

____

Small Wins:

____

CHAPTER LXXXIII

Day 83

"In the end, we only regret the chances we didn't take." - tiny buddha

Morning Affirmations

Write 5 affirmations as you start the day. (A few suggestions for affirmations as below)

"I am worthy of success and abundance."
"I trust in the process of life."
"I release all fear and embrace confidence."

1. ____
2. ____
3. ____
4. ____
5. ____

Visualization & Intention Setting

Spend 5-10 minutes visualizing yourself as the confident, successful, abundant person you're becoming.

Today's Intentions:

1. ____
2. ____
3. ____

Gratitude Practice

List 3 things you're grateful for today:

1. ______________________________
2. ______________________________
3. ______________________________

Daily Action Towards Goals

What is one action you can take today that aligns with your goals?

____

Evening Reflection & Acknowledgment

How did you feel today? What did you accomplish? Any signs of manifestation?

____

Small Wins:

____

CHAPTER LXXXIV

Day 84

*"Let your dreams be bigger than your fears and
your actions louder than your words." – Unknown*

Morning Affirmations

Write 5 affirmations as you start the day. (A few suggestions for
affirmations as below)

"I am worthy of success and abundance."
"I trust in the process of life."
"I release all fear and embrace confidence."

1. ____
2. ____
3. ____
4. ____
5. ____

Visualization & Intention Setting

Spend 5-10 minutes visualizing yourself as the confident, successful,
abundant person you're becoming.

Today's Intentions:

1. ____
2. ____
3. ____

Gratitude Practice

List 3 things you're grateful for today:

1. _______________________________________
2. _______________________________________
3. _______________________________________

Daily Action Towards Goals

What is one action you can take today that aligns with your goals?

____

Evening Reflection & Acknowledgment

How did you feel today? What did you accomplish? Any signs of manifestation?

____

Small Wins:

____

CHAPTER LXXXV

Day 85

"Don't wait. The time will never be just right." — Napoleon Hill

Morning Affirmations

Write 5 affirmations as you start the day. (A few suggestions for affirmations as below)

"I am worthy of success and abundance."
"I trust in the process of life."
"I release all fear and embrace confidence."

1. _______________________________________
2. _______________________________________
3. _______________________________________
4. _______________________________________
5. _______________________________________

Visualization & Intention Setting

Spend 5-10 minutes visualizing yourself as the confident, successful, abundant person you're becoming.

Today's Intentions:

1. _______________________________________
2. _______________________________________
3. _______________________________________

Gratitude Practice

List 3 things you're grateful for today:

1. _______________________________________
2. _______________________________________
3. _______________________________________

Daily Action Towards Goals

What is one action you can take today that aligns with your goals?

____

Evening Reflection & Acknowledgment

How did you feel today? What did you accomplish? Any signs of manifestation?

____

Small Wins:

____

CHAPTER LXXXVI

Day 86

"Success usually comes to those who are too busy to be looking for it." — Henry David Thoreau

Morning Affirmations

Write 5 affirmations as you start the day. (A few suggestions for affirmations as below)

"I am worthy of success and abundance."
"I trust in the process of life."
"I release all fear and embrace confidence."

1. ____
2. ____
3. ____
4. ____
5. ____

Visualization & Intention Setting

Spend 5-10 minutes visualizing yourself as the confident, successful, abundant person you're becoming.

Today's Intentions:

1. ____
2. ____
3. ____

Gratitude Practice

List 3 things you're grateful for today:

1. _______________________________________
2. _______________________________________
3. _______________________________________

Daily Action Towards Goals

What is one action you can take today that aligns with your goals?

____

Evening Reflection & Acknowledgment

How did you feel today? What did you accomplish? Any signs of manifestation?

____

Small Wins:

____

CHAPTER LXXXVII

Day 87

"The difference between ordinary and extraordinary is that little extra." — Jimmy Johnson

Morning Affirmations

Write 5 affirmations as you start the day. (A few suggestions for affirmations as below)

"I am worthy of success and abundance."
"I trust in the process of life."
"I release all fear and embrace confidence."

1. ____
2. ____
3. ____
4. ____
5. ____

Visualization & Intention Setting

Spend 5-10 minutes visualizing yourself as the confident, successful, abundant person you're becoming.

Today's Intentions:

1. ____
2. ____
3. ____

Gratitude Practice

List 3 things you're grateful for today:

    1. ______________________________________

    2. ______________________________________

    3. ______________________________________

Daily Action Towards Goals

What is one action you can take today that aligns with your goals?

____

Evening Reflection & Acknowledgment

How did you feel today? What did you accomplish? Any signs of manifestation?

____

Small Wins:

____

Day 88

"Your limitation—it's only your imagination." –
Unknown

Morning Affirmations

Write 5 affirmations as you start the day. (A few suggestions for affirmations as below)
"I am worthy of success and abundance."
"I trust in the process of life."
"I release all fear and embrace confidence."

1. ____
2. ____
3. ____
4. ____
5. ____

Visualization & Intention Setting

Spend 5-10 minutes visualizing yourself as the confident, successful, abundant person you're becoming.

Today's Intentions:
1. ____
2. ____
3. ____

Gratitude Practice

List 3 things you're grateful for today:

1. _______________________________________
2. _______________________________________
3. _______________________________________

Daily Action Towards Goals

What is one action you can take today that aligns with your goals?

____

Evening Reflection & Acknowledgment

How did you feel today? What did you accomplish? Any signs of manifestation?

____

Small Wins:

____

CHAPTER LXXXIX

Day 89

"Hardships often prepare ordinary people for an extraordinary destiny." – C.S. Lewis

Morning Affirmations

Write 5 affirmations as you start the day. (A few suggestions for affirmations as below)
"I am worthy of success and abundance."
"I trust in the process of life."
"I release all fear and embrace confidence."

1. ____
2. ____
3. ____
4. ____
5. ____

Visualization & Intention Setting

Spend 5-10 minutes visualizing yourself as the confident, successful, abundant person you're becoming.
Today's Intentions:

1. ____
2. ____
3. ____

Gratitude Practice

List 3 things you're grateful for today:

1. _______________________________________
2. _______________________________________
3. _______________________________________

Daily Action Towards Goals

What is one action you can take today that aligns with your goals?

____

Evening Reflection & Acknowledgment

How did you feel today? What did you accomplish? Any signs of manifestation?

____

Small Wins:

____

Day 90

"The best preparation for tomorrow is doing your best today." — H. Jackson Brown, Jr.

Morning Affirmations

Write 5 affirmations as you start the day. (A few suggestions for affirmations as below)

"I am worthy of success and abundance."
"I trust in the process of life."
"I release all fear and embrace confidence."

1. ____
2. ____
3. ____
4. ____
5. ____

Visualization & Intention Setting

Spend 5-10 minutes visualizing yourself as the confident, successful, abundant person you're becoming.

Today's Intentions:

1. ____
2. ____
3. ____

Gratitude Practice

List 3 things you're grateful for today:

1. _______________________________________
2. _______________________________________
3. _______________________________________

Daily Action Towards Goals

What is one action you can take today that aligns with your goals?

____

Evening Reflection & Acknowledgment

How did you feel today? What did you accomplish? Any signs of manifestation?

____

Small Wins:

____

Day 91

"Motivation is what gets you started. Habit is what keeps you going." – Jim Rohn

Morning Affirmations

Write 5 affirmations as you start the day. (A few suggestions for affirmations as below)

"I am worthy of success and abundance."
"I trust in the process of life."
"I release all fear and embrace confidence."

1. ____
2. ____
3. ____
4. ____
5. ____

Visualization & Intention Setting

Spend 5-10 minutes visualizing yourself as the confident, successful, abundant person you're becoming.

Today's Intentions:

1. ____
2. ____
3. ____

Gratitude Practice

List 3 things you're grateful for today:

1. _______________________________
2. _______________________________
3. _______________________________

Daily Action Towards Goals

What is one action you can take today that aligns with your goals?

____

Evening Reflection & Acknowledgment

How did you feel today? What did you accomplish? Any signs of manifestation?

____

Small Wins:

____

Day 92

"Don't limit your challenges, challenge your limits." – Jerry Dunn

Morning Affirmations

Write 5 affirmations as you start the day. (A few suggestions for affirmations as below)

"I am worthy of success and abundance."
"I trust in the process of life."
"I release all fear and embrace confidence."

1. ____
2. ____
3. ____
4. ____
5. ____

Visualization & Intention Setting

Spend 5-10 minutes visualizing yourself as the confident, successful, abundant person you're becoming.

Today's Intentions:

1. ____
2. ____
3. ____

Gratitude Practice

List 3 things you're grateful for today:

1. _______________________________
2. _______________________________
3. _______________________________

Daily Action Towards Goals

What is one action you can take today that aligns with your goals?

____

Evening Reflection & Acknowledgment

How did you feel today? What did you accomplish? Any signs of manifestation?

____

Small Wins:

____

Day 93

"Believe in yourself and all that you are. Know that there is something inside you that is greater than any obstacle." – Christian D. Larson

Morning Affirmations

Write 5 affirmations as you start the day. (A few suggestions for affirmations as below)

"I am worthy of success and abundance."
"I trust in the process of life."
"I release all fear and embrace confidence."

1. ____
2. ____
3. ____
4. ____
5. ____

Visualization & Intention Setting

Spend 5-10 minutes visualizing yourself as the confident, successful, abundant person you're becoming.

Today's Intentions:

1. ____
2. ____
3. ____

Gratitude Practice

List 3 things you're grateful for today:

    1. ____

    2. ____

    3. ____

Daily Action Towards Goals

What is one action you can take today that aligns with your goals?

Evening Reflection & Acknowledgment

How did you feel today? What did you accomplish? Any signs of manifestation?

Small Wins:

Day 94

"Success is the result of preparation, hard work, and learning from failure." – Colin Powell

Morning Affirmations

Write 5 affirmations as you start the day. (A few suggestions for affirmations as below)
"I am worthy of success and abundance."
"I trust in the process of life."
"I release all fear and embrace confidence."

1. _______________________________________
2. _______________________________________
3. _______________________________________
4. _______________________________________
5. _______________________________________

Visualization & Intention Setting

Spend 5-10 minutes visualizing yourself as the confident, successful, abundant person you're becoming.

Today's Intentions:

1. _______________________________________
2. _______________________________________
3. _______________________________________

Gratitude Practice

List 3 things you're grateful for today:

1. ____
2. ____
3. ____

Daily Action Towards Goals

What is one action you can take today that aligns with your goals?

____

Evening Reflection & Acknowledgment

How did you feel today? What did you accomplish? Any signs of manifestation?

____

Small Wins:

____

Additional Resources

Focus Wheel Template

Focus Wheel

1. **Center Circle (Your Desire):**
   Write your main desire or goal in the center circle.
   Example: "I am confident and successful."
2. **Surrounding Circles (Positive Beliefs):**
   In the surrounding circles, write positive beliefs or thoughts that support your central desire. Aim for 6-8 statements.
   Examples:

   - "I attract opportunities effortlessly."
   - "I believe in my abilities."
   - "I am deserving of success."
   - "My confidence grows daily."
   - "I am surrounded by supportive people."
   - "I learn and grow from challenges."
   - "I take inspired action towards my goals."
   - "My past experiences prepare me for future success."

3. **Action Steps:**
   Below the focus wheel, list specific actions you can take to align with your desire.
   Examples:

   - Attend networking events.
   - Practice public speaking.
   - Read books on confidence and success.
   - Journal my daily achievements.

4. **Gratitude Statements:**
   Add a section for gratitude, where you write down what you're grateful for related to your desire.

Example:

- ◦ "I am grateful for my supportive friends."
- ◦ "I appreciate the opportunities I have."

• • •

How to Use the Focus Wheel

1. **Write Your Desire:**
   Clearly state your desire in the center circle.
2. **Fill in Positive Beliefs:**
   Think about beliefs that align with your desire and fill in the surrounding circles.
3. **Identify Action Steps:**
   List concrete actions that will help you move towards your desire.
4. **Practice Gratitude:**
   Regularly reflect on what you're grateful for in relation to your desire.

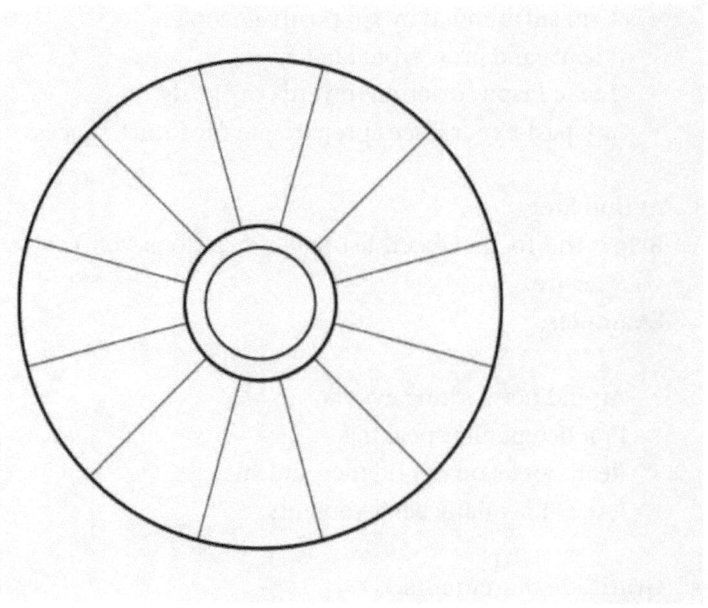

A focus wheel template for self-improvement and manifestation
exercises.

191

Ending Note

Congratulations on completing The 94-Day Ascension!

This journey was not just about filling pages, but about uncovering the most authentic, confident, and abundant version of yourself. Each day, you took a step toward aligning your thoughts, emotions, and actions with the life you desire. Now, as you look back at the past 94 days, I hope you can see how far you've come, the limiting beliefs you've released, and the new habits you've cultivated.

Remember, this is just the beginning. The tools and insights you've gained are yours to carry forward.

Thank you for allowing me to be part of your journey. Keep believing, keep rising, and always know that everything you seek is already within you.

With gratitude and light,
Neelima Davuluri